Trinity

by
Curtis Mischler

Sleeper Awakened, LLC Books are printed by Create Space and
are available for order through Ingram Press Catalogues.

This book is a work of fiction. Names, characters, places, and
incidents either are products of the author's imagination or are
used fictitiously. Any resemblance to actual persons, living or
dead, business establishments, events, or locales is entirely
coincidental.

Trinity

Visit my website at www.curtismischler.com

Printed in the United States of America
First Printing: May 2015
Published by Sleeper Awakened, LLC

ISBN: 978-1-62747-071-1
Ebook ISBN: 978-1-62747-072-8

Dedication

To my daughter, Maya. You inspire me every day. I am so happy to be your father. Please know that you can do anything that you decide to do. Keep growing. Keep exploring. I love you.

To Grandpa H. My namesake. You instilled in me a life-long love of science and exploration. My only regret is that you did not live long enough for us to have the science and philosophy discussions that I know we both would have deeply enjoyed. I think of you often.

Author's Note

This is a work of fiction. One that I hope you, as the reader, enjoy. Please note that the science presented in here is done for the sake of the story, not for the sake of science. This is both science fiction and "science" fiction.

Enjoy!

Chapter 1

T he desert stretched in all directions, as far as the eye could see. Desolate, barren, beautiful. Nothing was stirring, except for a hawk circling lazily overhead in the waning sunlight.

The few scrub brush and cacti cast long shadows in the diminishing light as night rapidly approached. Darkness was settling over the desert yet again.

It was very quiet and still. The occasional rustle of brush or cry of the hawk were the only sounds that disturbed this tranquil setting.

In a blinding instant, that calm was shattered by the light of a thousand suns. In that moment the universe shifted, both in time and space. Subtly, but measurably, if one knew where and how to look.

The desert sand beneath the growing mushroom cloud was instantaneously fused into radioactive glass. The shock wave rolled outward, knocking the hawk from the sky and blowing dust and debris for miles.

In a bunker several miles away, a team of scientists scurried like mice in a maze as they recorded and monitored the event.

"Mushroom cloud building as theorized." "Shock wave passing on schedule." "Nominal yield estimate at 17-20 kilotons." The reports continued on and on.

In the center of this mayhem stood a tall, thin, soft-spoken scientist, Dr. Wayne C. Howell. He had been part of the Manhattan project from the beginning, and his scientific excitement was impossible to escape. He was monitoring the event closely, but he had no idea as to the true impact of this event. The impact that it would have on him, on his family, and on the universe.

The world had just stepped into the nuclear age in the high desert of New Mexico. But with that step, a small tear was caused in the fabric of space and time. A tear that was undetectable by the instruments of that age. A tear that, based on his proximity, attached itself to Dr. Howell in his genetic code and would affect his future generations. And thus was set in motion a series of events that transcends time and space.

For time and space are everywhere and nowhere, everywhen and nowhen, all at the same time. Like the Heisenberg Uncertainty principle on a cosmic scale, we are all things at once. And none of them, too.

Dr. Howell put down his viewing glasses and stumbled back. He felt suddenly ill. He checked his radiation badge - it showed all clear. Radiation was always the first thought when one felt ill; it had claimed a number of scientists' lives along the way.

Dr. Howell turned to his nearest colleague, "Carl, do you feel different? Ill in any way?"

Dr. Carl Dietrich turned in his direction. "No, Wayne, I feel fine, other than a sense of awe, of accomplishment. Why, is something wrong?"

Wayne leaned against the instrument panel. "I'm not sure. I feel funny, like something isn't right, like I was part of the explosion, at the explosion." He paused, "but it seems to be passing. Perhaps it's today's lunch getting me back," he said with a wry smile.

At that point, Dr. Robert Oppenheimer, the director of the project, walked over. "Wayne, Carl, look at this!" he shouted above the din. "These readings are off the scale! We'll need months to analyze this data."

Carl leaned in over his shoulder, "What is this spike in theta range on the reading?"

"I don't know," Robert replied. "That is odd. Perhaps the sensors are off? Wayne, what do you think?"

There was no answer. "Wayne? Wayne?" The two scientists turned.

But Dr. Howell could not hear them. He had fallen to the floor in a trance.

Chapter 2

The physician checked the vitals one more time. "There is nothing physically wrong with him. Blood pressure, temperature, reflexes are all within norms. It is almost like his body is there, but not his soul."

He turned to the woman standing next to the bed. "Meredith, I'm sorry, but there is nothing we can do but wait."

Meredith looked down at her husband. It had been two weeks since the test, and he was still in the same trance. "May I stay and speak with him?" she asked the doctor.

"Of course. Take all the time you want." The doctor slipped out of the room and let her have some privacy.

Meredith sat down on the lone chair next to the bed. She looked around the room. A typical army hospital room; all stainless steel and brilliant white walls, tile floors, and government-issued bed and cabinets. It was all so stark, so cold. She involuntarily shivered.

Her husband of ten years lay there, still. His hawkish nose stood up in stark contrast to the bedding. She took his hand and leaned in to whisper in his ear.

"Wayne, it's Maggie." He had given her that nickname when they had started dating. She had completely forgotten where it came from, but only her husband and very close friends called her that. "I'm here. For as long as it takes. I didn't think I would ever find you before we met, and I'll be damned now if I won't find you again. Follow my voice and find your way home."

They had met on the train from Lecompton to the University of Kansas. They had each grown up in small Kansas towns where farming was the primary profession, and each had duties on their family farms that they juggled when not in school. That they had met was pure chance, but it changed both of their lives. They knew that they were destined for each other. She an undergraduate physics major, which was very unusual for a woman at the time, and he a graduate student in nuclear physics.

She leaned closer, "I'm ready to try again. Andrew being stillborn crushed both us, especially after all the miscarriages, but I'm not giving up. We don't give up."

She wiped away a tear. "I've seen our future, and it includes kids, grandkids, even great-grandkids. But I need you back to make that happen. So come back to me from wherever you are. And when you do, tell me about this journey that you have been on."

Meredith lowered her head onto her husband's chest and listened to the beating of his heart, to the rhythmic rise and fall of his breathing. She rested there and prayed as another tear streaked down her cheek. Wayne was her world, and she couldn't live in that world without him.

Chapter 3

T he cries rippled out to the corridor. Screams for air in lungs that had never breathed before.

"It's a girl. Perfect. Ten fingers, ten toes," the doctor smiled down at Meredith. "Shall I go get Wayne?"

"Please." Meredith took the baby in her arms. Her little miracle. After all the tries, the miscarriages, the stillbirth, here was a beautiful baby girl.

Wayne entered the room. "Maggie, you did it." The proud smile that spread across his face lit up the entire room. He bent down over his girls and gave his wife a kiss on her forehead and then did the same for his daughter.

Meredith looked him in the eyes and said, "Eleanor."

"Yes," he replied, "Eleanor. She's perfect."

Meredith smiled, "Yes, she is. Thank you for not giving up. For never giving up."

"I never could with you."

A nurse walked in the room. "It's time to rest for both of you. Dad can come with me to the nursery."

Wayne looked at Meredith, and she nodded her assent. "I would like to sleep anyway." The nurse gently picked up Eleanor and placed her in a bassinet. "Come with me, Dad," she said as she rolled the bassinet towards the door.

Meredith closed her eyes with a final, "Goodnight, dear," and she was asleep.

Wayne followed the nurse down the hall and watched through the glass as she wheeled Eleanor into position. "You beautiful, beautiful baby girl. My Eleanor. I never thought I would see this day." Tears began to slowly pour down his cheeks. "I will always be there for you, Eleanor. Always. You can count on me to support you in whatever you do, my beautiful girl."

A voice overhead announced it was time for visiting hours to end. Wayne took one last look at Eleanor and turned to go. He still had work to do at the lab.

He exited the hospital and headed for his car. It was near the back of the parking lot, but as he neared it, his senses began to fade. He stumbled the rest of the way to his car, managed to unlock it and sit down, and then he lurched forward into blinding light. The light of a million suns, with him at the center. He looked around but could see nothing in the brilliance. Yet, he could sense another presence. No, two other presences. They seemed familiar, as if he had known them his entire life.

He cried out, but no sound escaped his lips. He reached out, but his hands could feel only nothingness. He listened, but he could hear nothing. The light was brilliant, all-encompassing. It enveloped him, cradled him in its interior. He was wrapped up in its heat, in its accelerating nuclear chain reaction as it swelled outward and upward. He roared with it, as did the two other presences.

Words came into his mind but dissolved before he could grasp them. His body was tossed and battered, yet his soul was at peace. A warm, burning peace. At that moment, he was one with everything, with everyone. He completely gave in to this feeling and embraced the oneness. In so doing, he merged with the other two and could share their thoughts. He could see between them a connection. Strands of DNA twisting together in a web that extended infinitely back in time and forward as well. But at the point of the web where he was, there was a divergence. A splitting of the web that spread farther apart the further it went into the future. The other two lay along that path, and he could see that the web would split, would fall apart in the future. Indeed, it already was. He could see it falling, unraveling, and in so doing traveling back up in reverse, pulling the whole web apart. The very fabric of existence. He watched in horror as everything disintegrated around him. And in that last moment as it all went dark, he entered complete nothingness.

When he awoke, it was dark outside the window. He struggled to sit up. His watch said it was nearly two in the morning. He'd lost just over eight hours. Where had it gone? Wayne shook his head, and the aftereffects of his vision slowly cleared.

The scientist that he was took an objective look at what had happened. One after another he eliminated possible scenarios. In the end, the only explanation that made sense was that he had had another event like the one at the first atomic bomb test.

Wayne started the car and headed to his lab. He was surprised to see the lights were still on. He showed his badge to the guard to gain entry. "Good evening, Dr. Howell. Dr. Dietrich is still up there; he's been up there all night, Sir."

Wayne nodded and headed up the stairs to the Nuclear Research lab. It took up the whole second floor of the building and was the main workspace for him and Carl.

When he walked in, Carl looked up excitedly. "You're not going to believe this, Wayne. Remember those readings from Trinity? The ones we couldn't explain and could never reproduce? Well, approximately eight hours ago, the sensors picked up the same thing again. Localized near here. Check out the graph there; you can see the distribution in energy levels at the upper registers."

Wayne looked at the points where Carl was marking the graph. "That does look the same. When, exactly, did it spike?"

Carl checked the time stamp. "The phenomenon started at 6:03 p.m. and built to maximum sustained intensity at 6:43. It then lasted for 10 minutes before dropping completely off at 7:03. I have been monitoring continually since then. Nothing further has shown up."

Wayne sat weakly on his stool. "Carl, I just had another hallucination, like the one I experienced at

Trinity, which started just about the same time. But it lasted hours. I came straight here after I came to."

Carl ran from the room and came back a moment later with an instrument tray. "Let me hook these up to you. EKG, oscilloscope, etc." Carl's hands flew as they hooked up the devices.

Results began to squiggle on paper as it rolled off the machines. Zigzag, zigzag. Beep, beep, beep, beep. Carl took a pencil and started marking data on the pages. "Hmmmm, a peak here, a valley there," he murmured to himself.

"It appears that you have a spike in the upper theta waves. I would like to try something." Carl took a Geiger counter off the shelf, switched it on, and it started emitting the familiar low static sound it is known for. He waved it over himself, and there was no change in static level. He did the same with Wayne, and still there was no change.

He went to the lead-lined safe and pulled out a chunk of rock. "Uranium ore, unrefined, but it should do." When Carl waved the Geiger counter over the rock, the distinctive click-clack sound indicating the presence of radiation sounded forth.

"Wayne, I want you to hold the rock." Wayne picked it up and Carl waved the Geiger counter over the rock in Wayne's outstretched hand. There was no elevation in static level, indicating that there was no radiation present. Wayne looked at Carl, "how is that possible?"

"It appears that you are somehow absorbing the radiation. Like you are a radiation sink, almost like a black hole for radiation." Carl sat down. "Now, bear with me. I think your episode at the Trinity test, as well as the one tonight, are somehow related to your elevated theta levels and this corresponding effect as a radiation sink. We need to go back to the Trinity site and see what we can find. It certainly appears that that is where this all started."

"But it's closed to everyone now, even us."

"Yes, but we have to find a way," Carl paused. "Are you familiar with the work that Norm Kaminski has been doing since Trinity? It is all theoretical, of course, but he points to the possibility of a fracture in space-time caused by an event such as a nuclear explosion. This theoretical fracture could link dimensions like a kind of bridge, or it could do the opposite and destroy the links between worlds; between time and existence. If that is what happened, and you are somehow connected to it, we need to know. It could even be at the cellular level. It could have changed your DNA."

"Eleanor!" gasped Wayne. He looked wildly at Carl. "My daughter, she was just born. I'm not sure when she was conceived, but it could have been either right before or just after the Trinity test. Could I have somehow passed this on to her?"

"I don't know. We need to talk to Norm, and we need to get to Trinity. At once, let's go."

The two scientists, friends, rose together. "Carl, thank you for your help, whatever may happen next." And the two headed for the door.

Chapter 4

C ris, age seven, rolled over in bed, not asleep, not ready to wake up on a Saturday morning. In that semi-dream state between waking and sleeping, he listened to the stillness of the house. The branches of the tree outside his bedroom window slowly swayed in the breeze, occasionally lightly brushing the window. Saturday morning, his favorite time of the week. Sleep in a bit, and then get up to watch cartoons. Lazy Saturday!

His reverie was shaken by a shout coming up the stairs and echoing down the hallway, "Eleanor, Wayne is dead!"

His heart stopped as the shout reverberated in his ears. Wayne. Dead. His grandfather. This could not be! Grandpa had just come back from the hospital the night before. The heart valve surgery had gone well. They had thrown a party to welcome him home and celebrate.

No, this could not be real. It must be a dream. He was not fully awake yet, so he must have dreamt it. Certainly if he stayed in bed, it would not be real. No, his grandpa had to be just fine.

His grandfather, who had taught him Morse code in their long walks through the woods, taught him how to throw a boomerang and not get hit on the return, taught him to see the modern wonders of the world all around him. His grandfather, who opened up and encouraged his interest in science. An interest shared always, with him. Cris knew that Grandpa had been a nuclear physicist, but he was too young to understand all of that. He was only seven, after all. He yearned for the day when he could have real conversations with his grandpa. About the atom, creation, the bomb, the work Grandpa had done during World War II. All the questions to which he knew he needed to be old enough to understand the answers, that he was waiting to ask when he was older and it was the right moment.

"Grandpa," slipped through Cris's lips. He knew it was real, even though he couldn't accept it. Cris slipped out of bed and slowly walked his way down the stairs. His brother and sister were watching cartoons. His mom, dad, and grandma were back in the guest room. Where Grandpa was.

Mom walked out, and Cris could see it in her face. She said, "Cristian, your grandpa died in his sleep last night." Tears rolled down her face. Cris's heart sank into a small, dark spot.

He looked at his mom. "Can I see him?" he asked.

Cris hesitantly walked into the guest room. He could hear his grandma wailing in the bathroom, pure anguish pouring out of her. He stepped to the side of the bed. A sheet covered his grandpa from head to toe. He pulled it back and saw his grandfather lying there with his mouth open in a silent gasp. His head was arched back, and his hands looked as though they were trying to grab something. Cris touched him. He felt so cold – so cold. Not how a person was supposed to feel. That made it real. Grandpa was gone.

As he turned to leave, he saw a glimmer of something at the edge of his eye. He turned to look, but it was gone. He paused for a moment, and then walked out of the house and into the backyard.

He stared up at the sky. Blue, sunny, clouds lazily passing by. How could something so beautiful exist on the day when his grandpa died? He looked at the grass, the trees swinging in the breeze. He felt a sense of loss, but he could not cry. The tears would not come. He sat down and let himself fall inward, to nothingness.

Later that night, it hit him like a crumpling blow. Grandpa was gone! The tears then started and flowed heavily down his face. His body racked with sobs. He couldn't stop crying, could not control the emotions flowing out from him. He distantly sensed arms around him, telling him it would be okay. He nestled in and let the tears flow freely. Missing his grandpa. He had always had a special connection there, and he felt that loss as much as anything. His dream of growing up a scientist with his grandpa was gone. He cried and cried.

But there was something else missing, too. He couldn't place it, but something did not feel right. As though this was not supposed to have happened. That his grandpa had left too soon. He could not explain it, but at the core of his being, he knew this to be true: this was wrong! And he needed to know why and what he could do about it.

He fell asleep crying in his mother's arms. His dreams that night carried him through time and space. Far across the void. He did not remember his dreams the next day. But if he had, he would have seen both his past and his future. They would come to him another day.

Chapter 5

Maya rolled out of bed and sat there. The dream had disturbed her. She had seen her dad as a child, age seven like she was, and he had been crying. She had also seen a man she thought was her great-grandpa.

She padded into her parents' room and snuggled between them. Her dad opened one eye and said, "Hey, little one. How are you?"

She smiled and gave him a hug. "Dad, can I ask you a question?"

"You just did," he said with a smile.

"Dad," she said, drawing out the word with an exasperated tone. "Another one. What was Great-Grandpa Howell like?"

He paused, "Why do you ask? Did you have a dream about him?"

"I did. You were in it, too. As a kid, like me."

"Tell me about it."

"Well, you were crying. And Grandma was there, holding you. I saw a man standing there, watching, and I think he was Great-Grandpa Howell."

Cris looked at his daughter "I had a similar dream last night, too. You want to know about my grandpa?"

"Yes," she nodded.

"Well, he was a lovely man. Kind, generous, tall. And very smart. He was a scientist; he studied the universe and the atom. I loved him very much. He grew up in Kansas where he met my grandma - your grandma's mom. He worked on the atomic bomb and for the Naval Research Laboratory. He was very kind, Grandpa. I loved him very much."

"What would you do with him?"

"He taught me how to throw a boomerang. He taught me how to talk on a ham radio. He had such great radios! And a big radio tower in his backyard. He could speak to people all over the world from there. I loved going to visit him in the summer in Kansas. I would spend two whole weeks there."

"I wish I could have met him. He sounds nice."

"He would have loved you, he truly would have."

"Thanks, Daddy," and with a kiss, she bounded out the room and down the stairs.

Cris rolled over to his wife, Jennifer. "I had the dream again, and this time she did, too."

"What does it mean?"

"I'm not sure, but I was warned this could happen. Sooner than I expected. But if it is really happening, we need to get ready. I have Grandpa's papers. I'll go over them again, what I can understand, at least, and see if there is anything we can do."

Cris kissed Jennifer and headed down the hall to his study. Posters lined the walls - space, aircraft, astronauts - the life he had always wanted, but could not have because of his height. Curse being so tall! He lost his way when he couldn't be an astronaut, and while he was successful, it felt hollow because it was not his calling.

Cris sat in his chair and wondered if his grandfather's death may have also played a part in that. His love of science endured, but it was a bit sad after Grandpa was gone. It had slowly faded away.

He looked at his grandpa's lab stool, sitting there next to the desk. He imagined his grandpa sitting on that stool and discovering the mysteries of the universe. He reached out and gave it a twirl. The sound was comforting.

He reached to the shelf and pulled down the binders that were left for him when his grandma died. These binders had the remaining papers that Grandpa had published. There was also a note for Cris that said these would be very important someday, and that he would understand when that was.

Unfortunately, that day had not yet come. He opened the binders and began to read again. The first paper had to do with static electricity discharge from aircraft. Not the most engaging topic for a nonscientist, but Cris plunged ahead anyway. As he did, he noticed that certain passages were marked. He looked closely at them, but could discern no special relevance. He moved on.

The next paper was on the moment right after a critical mass is obtained in a nuclear reaction. Cris could understand some of it from his college math and science, but much of it was over his head. In the margin next to one particularly complicated equation was the word "dreams" in what he thought was his grandpa's writing. He paused at that. Dreams. What could that mean?

He turned on the monitor and pulled up Google. "Let's see if I can find this equation anywhere," he muttered to himself. He typed it in and voila, several results came up. Wikipedia he skipped, and scrolled down. There was one for the Naval Research Lab, where his grandpa had been the director for several years. He clicked on that link. Up popped a summary for the Kaminski Time-Space equation. He looked at it more closely. It described the effects of intense radiation, a singularity, and the potential for a rip in space-time.

Cris paused. His physics was rusty, but he knew that singularities occurred at the center of black holes. What did that have to do with this?

He pulled an old textbook off the shelf and turned to the section on singularities. He read the chapter. And the next. And the next. Then something caught his eye. "Singularities are also created at the instant that a nuclear weapon is detonated. They only last for a microsecond, but in that time, they are real. The only known occurrence of a manmade singularity."

He set the book down in his lap. A singularity. With high doses of radiation. He thought to himself, *Could this be what Grandpa was trying to tell me?*

He knew his grandpa had somehow been part of the early nuclear weapons programs, the Manhattan Project and beyond, but he had never been able to discuss it with him. He had been too young when his grandpa died.

Was it possible that something had happened at one of the tests? Was it possible that Kaminski's theory was real?

Cris Googled Norm Kaminski and found that he was a professor emeritus at Princeton University, with doctorates in both theoretical and applied physics. He had been published many times over, with most of his papers focused on the effects of nuclear reactions on space and time.

He sat back. Princeton was just up the road from Philadelphia; perhaps it was time to go see Professor Kaminski.

Chapter 6

T he train ride to Princeton was a short one, not more than an hour. More and more, Cris was using public transportation as he settled into life on the east coast. He sat back and watched the countryside go by. Occasional farmland, horses, but mostly urban.

He closed his eyes and rubbed them. He didn't know where this journey was headed, but he was determined to find out. As he rocked to the gentle swaying of the train, he suddenly felt a sensation of falling. Of falling back. Of falling in.

Everything was caught in a searing light. Blinding, all around him. He could sense the heavens reeling, birthing, dying all around him. He felt a oneness with everything. A brilliant point of light grew to giant proportions and engulfed everything. He was the light. He was everything.

He sensed another presence with him. Someone older, kind. He could not see this person, but he knew he was there. He tried to shout out, but nothing would come. His heart beat faster and faster. There was something here; someone here with whom he was supposed to connect, but he couldn't.

He let himself go with the tidal forces throwing him around on the cosmic breeze. He relaxed and extended his arms and legs in the brilliance around him. He felt the other presence do the same, and they came together. One, yet distinct.

In that brief moment, he caught a glimpse of something; something very familiar. Something he had sensed that day in his grandpa's room when he said his last goodbye. He reached for it, and it was there. And he knew who it was.

He began to understand. That everything and everyone is connected, yet we rarely see that in our own worlds as me move from moment to moment, day to day. There is the possibility of "bigger"; of recognizing and feeling and exploring the connections, throughout the universe and across time and space. If only he could learn to control it....

But there was something else; something wrong. He could sense the universe unraveling around him. It was not right, he could feel that to his core. He didn't understand it all, but he knew that if this could not be stopped, could not be repaired, that the universe was in danger of falling apart.

With a rush of light and cosmic wind, he was thrust violently back into the real world. On the train. Pulling into New York City. He had missed his stop in Princeton. He'd have to get off and get the next train headed south.

As he stepped off, one word escaped his lips, "Grandpa."

When Cris finally arrived at Princeton University, he went straight to the physics department. The receptionist greeted him politely and asked how she could help.

"I'm looking for Professor Norm Kaminski," Cris stated.

"I'm sorry, but the professor no longer sees students," she replied

"But I'm not a student. This is a personal matter."

"I'm sorry, but you need an appointment. Please give me your information and I will call you with his next availability."

"This is urgent. I need to speak with him. Please, isn't there anything you can do?"

"I'm sorry, but rules are rules. Please fill out this card and I will pass it on."

Before Cris could reply, a small, white-haired gentleman shuffled into the room. He looked Cris up and down, and then waved for him to follow as he shuffled back from where he had entered.

Cris looked at the receptionist. She had an expression that indicated she did not approve, but she nodded for him to go on.

Cris caught up to the old man. "Thank you for getting me past that point. I'm looking for Professor Kaminski."

"Well, you've found him, young man, you've found him. You do look like him, you know."

"Who?"

"Why, your grandfather, of course. Wayne Cristian Howell. Come this way."

The professor led them into a small lab and sat down in a chair. He waved Cris over to one of the stools and motioned for him to sit down. "Now, why is it that you have finally come?"

Cris pulled his grandfather's papers from his bag. "It's your equation on time-space fracture and this note about dreams." He handed it over to the professor's waiting hand. "You knew my grandfather well?"

"Yes, you could say that. We came up together on the Manhattan Project, among other things. Let me see what we have here." He paged through the documents, skimming over the notes and equations. "Yes, yes, the dream corollary, of course."

He turned to Cris with a hard stare and asked, "Have you had moments where you lose awareness of your surroundings?"

"Yes, in fact it happened again on the train ride up here. I was out for an hour or two."

"I see, and is the frequency of these events changing in anyway?"

"I don't know. I don't really track them."

"Well, you must! From now on, I want you to log every one of these events. Time, place, duration, significant memories that remain behind. This could be very important. Why did you come to see me today?"

"My daughter and I had the same dream last night, and I...."

"What? Your daughter, how old is she?"

"Seven"

"And how old were you when your grandfather died?"

"I was also seven."

"Hmmm, interesting. And disturbing, yet very interesting. Sit back, I'm going to tell you a story about three young scientists that may have great import to what you are describing.

"In the summer of 1945, we were all assigned to the Manhattan Project. Your grandfather, Carl Dietrich, and me. We each had different specializations, but we were put in the same lab as there was not much space to go around at Los Alamos. The three of us hit it off immediately. We became three peas in a pod. We did everything together, even though that usually involved theoretical nuclear physics." Norm stopped to chuckle. "We worked around the clock. Not because of the war effort, but because of the science! We were breaking barriers, going where no one had been before.

"Your grandfather was a sharp mind. He postulated many of the effects of the nuclear device we were building, and Carl and I extrapolated much of that into our own equations. One of which is the time-space fracture equation. You see, at the moment of a nuclear detonation, it is like the Big Bang and a black hole, all at once. A singularity is created, but not naturally, and that is the key. Some things are not supposed to happen, and I believe that this is one of them.

"But we didn't care at the time. We were young scientists chasing the truth! Nothing could stop us! We would persevere! I still remember to this day the original test. Out in the New Mexico desert. It was amazing, awesome power that we unleashed that day.

But we had gotten a little ahead of ourselves and did not fully appreciate, nor understand, what we were unleashing.

"I do believe that a rip occurred that day. The conditions were right for it. But I also believe, and this is where most scientists call me a fool, but I was there! I saw it! I believe that this rip somehow attached itself to your grandfather at the molecular level. It could have happened to any one of us, but he was, as they say, in the right place at the right time.

"I think this rip changed his genetic structure ever so slightly. It brought him in tune with the cosmos in a very different way from the rest of us. And I believe that it could be passed genetically to his heirs. Based on what you are describing, I think that is exactly what happened!"

"Now, as to dreams, I believe this rip provides a means to jump time and space - forward, backward, up, down, across multiple dimensions. Dreams have often been theorized to be portals to other dimensions, so it would make sense for there to be a dream aspect to this as well. If that is true, it should be possible for you to jump through space and time, and I think that is what is happening when you have your little 'hallucinations.'"

The professor paused and a grim smile spread across his face. "However, there is a theoretical downside to all of this. And that is that the rip continues to grow with successive generations. To the point that the very fabric of space and time is torn asunder. In other words, it could bring the end of the universe as we know it.

"Appropriate in a perverse way that a weapon that threatens our very existence here on Earth could mean the same for all creation." The professor paused, "so that is the ultimate question. Are we headed down a path of assured destruction or can it be stemmed? That, my young friend, is a question that you will be forced to face, whether you like it or not."

He paused to look at Cris. Cris was sitting there with a blank look, taking it all in. This was a lot to process all at once. He looked up, "What about my daughter?"

"Based on the dream you described, it is very likely that she is experiencing some of the same effects that you are. It also seems curious that this is happening at the same age as when your grandfather passed. Likely a cruel cosmic joke, but still very real."

"What about my brother and sister and their kids? They don't seem to have any effects?"

"Hmmm, that is interesting. You were the closest to your grandfather, correct? And you are the oldest child of his oldest child? And Maya is your oldest child?" Cris nodded yes to all three questions. "Then it is likely that there is an aspect of this that is tied to that. Perhaps the oldest child in each generation is more attuned to the effects. Regardless, it is true that you are having them, and we need to do something about it."

"What do you suggest?"

"For now, log your events. Record them. Do the same for your daughter. Beyond that, I don't know. I'll have to think on that and get back to you."

Chapter 7

W ayne stood up from the microscope and sighed. It had been a long day in the lab. His lab. As the associate director of the Naval Research Laboratory, he was responsible for overseeing much of the work done here.

He looked around at the various instruments and stations arrayed around the room. Modern by current standards, but soon to be obsolete based on the pace of the progress they were making.

One perk of his position was that he could pick his own areas of research. And his primary one continued to be what had happened that day so many years ago in New Mexico. Fortunately, the "events" as he liked to call them were happening less frequently. Almost as if they were directly related to the half-life of the atomic explosion that had triggered the first one.

It was still not clear what had happened that day, but he and Carl were working closer to that every day. He glanced at the clock. He needed to get back home to his family - his wife and two daughters. But he was too engaged right now with his research. Maggie would understand; she always did.

"Carl, let's try that sequence again," he called across the lab.

"Right, let me set the laser again."

They were trying to recreate the conditions from the Trinity site in the lab, without a nuclear reaction, of course. They were making progress, but it was slow, and much of it was hard to see.

"Wayne, we should be good to go. Let's use rock sample 4F1 this time."

Wayne loaded the rock in the apparatus. The samples were all from the Trinity site, and with the use of the laser, they could recreate most of the effects from the initial nuclear test without an actual nuclear reaction. So far they had been able to explain most of the sensor readings from that day.

Carl initiated the laser and it fired into the rock. Gases were expelled as the rock was heated. Sensors recorded the event in minute detail. At the three-minute mark, Carl shut off the laser and turned the lights back on.

"That should do it. Let's see what we've got!" He pulled the data from the nearest monitor. "There! See the beta waves? That should take care of that last missing piece."

Wayne swiveled on his stool back to the original readouts. "Confirmed, that takes care of the beta region. So only the theta effects are unexplained."

Carl took off his safety glasses. "The only way we're going to be able to measure theta levels is with an actual test."

"I know. The next one is on Eniwetok Atoll. We should go."

"The Marshall Islands? I hear they are beautiful this time of year," Carl responded with a smile.

The B-29 bumped and tossed with the weather as it descended to the makeshift base in the Marshall Islands. This was where all coordination was being done for the hydrogen bomb tests on Eniwetok Atoll.

The original Trinity device, as well as the bombs dropped on Japan (Fat Man and Little Boy), were atom bombs. They operated by nuclear fission, where atoms are split. In those devices, the atomic material was uranium or plutonium.

With an H-bomb, or hydrogen bomb, hydrogen was the element of choice. And rather than fission, fusion, or the combining of atoms, was the primary method driving the nuclear reaction and subsequent yield.

An H-bomb was several orders of magnitude larger than an atom bomb. The results would not be exactly the same, but Wayne and Carl had theoretically predicted what the effects should be. They had extrapolated the results from the Trinity site and would be able to compare them to Eniwetok.

Eniwetok was a tiny atoll in the Marshall Islands. It was selected for its remote location and lack of indigenous population. The thought was that no one would miss a small island once it was blown off the surface of the planet.

While extrapolation was not ideal, it was the only real option available. Atom bombs were no longer being built or tested, as the military favored the higher yield hydrogen bombs. So, in the field of nuclear weapons, this was the only place to be.

Wayne and Carl had been assigned to the telemetry division, so they would have access to all of the data as it came through. And they had predicted the results they needed to look for.

After dropping their bags at their barracks, they headed straight for the main data station. They had a lot to do to prepare for the next test, "Mike," which was scheduled for later that month. Not only did they have to setup all the equipment needed for measuring the actual effects of the H-bomb detonation, they also had to be prepared to measure the effects on Wayne. Neither scientist could be certain that anything like what happened in New Mexico would happen again, but they had to be ready. Nuclear detonations continued to be rare events.

When the day finally came, Wayne and Carl were in the bunker and ready to go well in advance of the test schedule. As the clock slowly wound down, they tuned the various instruments available to them: seismographs, oscilloscopes, thermometers, and other recording equipment. They also reviewed their own calculations one last time so they would be sure of what to look for, although that last step wasn't really necessary - they had the math committed to memory.

Wayne looked over to Carl. "Thank you for making this journey with me."

"Of course, I wouldn't be anywhere else at this moment. Are you ready?"

"As ready as I'll ever be." Wayne attached the last electrode to his chest. "Not only will we be able to monitor the bomb, we'll also be able to monitor me."

The loudspeaker in the room announced the final countdown, all personnel to stations, and all safety goggles in place.

The metallic voice intoned "10 ... 9 ... 8 ... 7 ..."

Wayne looked out the bunker in anticipation. He checked the monitors and saw what looked like a person standing near the device.

"5 ... 4 ..."

"Carl!" he shouted, "Do you see that?"

Carl glanced at the monitor, "See what?"

"2 ..."

And in the microsecond before the device detonated, Wayne's world went completely white. He looked around and he could see himself, another man, and a woman, all standing around the device.

The woman looked at him and said. "This is it, Great-Grandpa".

Before he could respond, the device detonated, and in that very first instant, they were all in the singularity together. They were one with the universe and one with each other.

"Do you see it?" said the woman. "If you look, you can see in all directions - in space, in time. They are all there before us."

Wayne asked, "How is this possible?"

"Because space and time are one, and they are everywhere and everywhen at once. We are able to see that, but we are the only ones – right, Daddy?"

Wayne turned to the other man. "Daddy?" he asked? "If you are her father, and I am her great-grandfather, that makes you ..."

"Your grandson Cristian. Named after you. Eleanor's firstborn," Cris smiled at his grandfather.

The woman interjected. "We don't have time for this now. We need to connect, as the very fabric of space-time is at risk. If we don't act soon, it will be too late."

"Soon?" asked Wayne.

"I understand that *soon* is a relative concept. Especially with space-time. We are everywhen at once, yet there is still an inescapable march of time through the cosmos. And that march is heading towards a cliff that spells certain disaster. If we don't stop it, it will be the end of the universe. I can't hold us in this moment much longer - I have to let go. But we need to meet again at the next H-bomb test, and at that point we will have to fix the rift."

"The rift that was created at the Trinity site during the first atomic bomb test, the rift that, for whatever reason, focused on our string of the cosmic web, on our DNA. But only ours. I don't know why, but that is the case. This rift, while giving us the ability to jump through time and space within our genetic line, also represents a serious threat to the universe. It could spell the end of the universe if we don't close it soon. And the next opportunity to do that is at the next hydrogen bomb test. We can't reuse the same points in time again, as we would end up in a cosmic loop, so we must move from singularity to singularity, from nuclear event to nuclear event, and we are running out of them. The next test is the one."

In the next instant, the singularity exploded outward, and Wayne was thrown back into his body. He opened his eyes to see Carl staring at him.

"Are you okay?"

"Why?"

"At the moment of detonation, all your vital signs stopped. It was as if you weren't here. You can see them on the monitor. It was only for a second or two, but you can definitely see it on the readings."

Wayne looked at the giant mushroom cloud towering above them. "Carl, I was gone, but it felt like 15 minutes. I was at the device upon detonation. With my grandson and great-granddaughter."

Carl looked at Wayne, "How is that possible?"

"I don't know. What were the theta levels?"

Carl took a moment to check, and a low whistle emanated from his mouth. "You are not going to believe this. They were three times higher than we predicted."

"Three times. And there were three of us. Any connection?"

"I don't know - that is beyond my field of expertise. We should bring in Kaminski on this."

"I agree. And I'm concerned, because my descendants gave me a warning. That unless we do something to stop it, we could be heading for the end of the universe."

Maya stood up from the stool and stretched her arms over her head. She looked down at her great-grandpa's stool. It only seemed appropriate that she would use it in her lab. It stunned her to think about how much science that stool had seen.

At only thirty-four, Dr. Maya Manning was the world's foremost expert on space-time theory. After undergrad at Michigan (U of M, not that other school!), she had completed her PhD at MIT and postdoctoral fellowships at Oxford and Stanford. She now ran her own lab out of the Smithsonian, yet it was largely funded by private donations. She didn't pay much attention to that as she was too busy with her research.

Her research that focused on bridging the space-time continuum and creating portals between dimensions. Theoretical physics had long held that this was possible, but nearly all models indicated that it was not a practical reality.

Maya disagreed, and her research was nearing the ability to do just that - jump dimensions and space-time. But she was finding one theoretical barrier that was proving impossible to get over.

It had to do with the genetic makeup of humans (and other creatures) and the finite place in space-time that DNA occupied. It appeared that DNA would have to flex in a certain way for jumps to be possible, and DNA just wasn't built to do that.

Multiple tests with mice, flies, and other smaller creatures had proven disheartening. None of the experiments were able to get past this theoretical barrier.

Maya sighed. She was so close, yet it felt like the final solution was a million light years away. Perhaps this was not meant to happen.

She walked from the room. When she felt the most frustrated, she found a walk or run the best way to clear her head. She didn't feel like running today, so she headed out for a quick walk around the campus.

As she did, her stress melted away. The cold air filled her lungs and cleared her head. Her long legs provided a rhythmic movement that lulled her thinking mind into a kind of trance, and she was able to let her mind wander. Various thoughts came to her. Most of these she let pass through her, but one remained: the dream she had when she was seven. She had had others since then, but none as intense or as closely coupled with her father. Why was that?

The question stuck with her as she made her way back across the yard. A thought jumped into her mind about the time-space fracture theorem. That had never been proven, but what if there was another way of looking at it?

She bounded up the steps two at a time and entered the foyer. The security guard looked up. "Package came for you while you were out, Dr. Manning."

"Really? I wasn't expecting anything. Thanks, Roger." She took the package and headed up the stairs to the lab. When she entered, she set down the package and looked it over. No return address, heavy, brown postal wrapping. It would have already been through normal security review before it made it to her, so she had no concerns opening it.

Inside was a small lead container labeled *Trinity*. Inside, she found a small rock with a note that said, "It all started here, and you'll find that your DNA is the key". There was no signature.

She looked at the wrapping again. Upon second review, it looked quite old – 100 years or more. That was odd. Her name and address were correct. She made a mental note to save it and see if someone in the carbon dating lab could tell her more.

She picked up the rock and put it in the spectrometer. It identified it as Trinitite, but no longer radioactive. Trinitite, created at the Trinity site during the first nuclear bomb test. Why did someone send this to her?

She read the note again. "It all started here, and you'll find that your DNA is the key." DNA; her daily struggle to find the key. On a whim, she pulled a hair and went to put it in the electron microscope. With advances over the years, electron microscopes could now see down to the level of DNA. She tried to bring it into focus, but could not. The image remained blurry.

She switched to a previous lab sample and tried again. This time, it worked perfectly and came straight into focus. *Odd*, she thought. She tried her hair again with the same effect. Next, she extracted some of her blood and tried that, too. Same results. No matter what she tried, it would not focus.

She collected her samples and headed down the hall to the biology physics lab. They had a 3D DNA microscope that should be able to resolve this. Dr. Kent Richards, the head of the biology department, was in the lab, and he agreed to help her with the sample.

He tried them both, and then leaned back in his chair. "Maya, where did you get these samples?"

"Why? Is there something wrong with them?"

"I don't know if I would say wrong, but I would say different. It appears that they are vibrating. That is why they won't come into focus. We'd have to calibrate the machine to vibrate with them in order to get a clear image."

"Vibrating? Is that even possible?"

"Evidently. It seems like the DNA in these samples are not locked in space. They appear to be moving back and forth very rapidly, almost as if they are in multiple dimensions at once."

Maya stood and looked out the window. Her DNA was the key.... But why was her DNA different? And what to do about it? Perhaps it was time for a trip up to Philly to see her parents again. It would be good to see them, and to check out their DNA.

Chapter 8

C ris sat down at his desk. Another long, stressful day was coming to a close. He looked out the window and let his mind wander. Would his days be as stressful if he had continued down the scientific path like his grandfather? Or was he just destined to be stressed all the time? He wondered about that.

He looked down at his messages. The standard ones from throughout the day. A problem with this, a problem with that. He tossed them aside; they could wait until tomorrow.

The last one caught his full attention. It was from Maya. She had her flights for Thanksgiving break and would be flying home from Michigan a day earlier than planned.

Cris smiled to himself; Jennifer would be thrilled! He read down further. Maya asked if he could pick her up at the airport alone, she wanted to talk with him about something, just the two of them.

He gazed out the window. What was bothering her? Nothing had come up in their weekly calls. Knowing Maya, if she wanted to discuss something, she would. He guessed that he would find out when the time was right.

On his drive home, he thought about Maya and Jennifer and the life they had together. They were as close as the three could be, yet there was a special bond that Maya had separately with each of her parents. Each was different, but unique to that parent. With his wife, it was always the relationship and emotional type issues that were covered. If Maya wasn't getting along with a friend, it was her mom she wanted. For him, it was the larger struggles to set a course, to do well, to be competitive. When Maya had issues with coursework or what classes to take next, it was her dad she wanted.

He wondered if anything was happening at school that would bother her. As far as he could tell, things were going well with her chosen major: architecture. She had interned at a prestigious New York City firm over the summer, and she only had three more semesters after this one before she would graduate. As long as he could remember, Maya wanted to be an architect.

He focused on the rest of his drive home knowing that he would see her in a few short days.

Chapter 9

C ris was at the airport well before Maya's flight
landed. He missed his little girl, even though she
wasn't so little anymore. An even six feet tall and
twenty-one years old, but he still saw his little girl when
he looked at her.

She came bounding out of the security gate and
gave him a big hug. "I missed you, Daddy!" His heart
melted every time she said "Daddy." It was much less
frequent now; usually, she just used "Dad," but on
those occasions when she really opened up, it was
"Daddy." Just the way he liked it.

He looked her over. "You look good, dear. College
isn't treating you too badly."

She gave a half smile. "No, college isn't, but there
are some other things I'd like to talk with you about.
Can we get a coffee on the way home?"

"Coffee? Since when do you drink coffee?" Cris
shook his head. "Of course, we can. Let's go get your
bags and we'll stop by a cafe on the way."

After they had settled into their chairs, each with a
medium roast, Maya started to open up.

"Dad, you know I've wanted to be an architect my whole life, right?"

"Yes"

"Well, I think it might be a different version of that than I originally thought."

"Go on. What do you mean?"

"Don't get me wrong, I love architecture. Always have, always will. But some things have been happening lately, and I'm starting to see things in a different light."

"Things? Are the dreams coming back?"

"Yes, they are. But it is more than that. I see more in them now. And I have more control within them. I sense an order to the whole thing. Symmetry. Almost as if things are planned, designed, built. Like architecture, but on a different scale, a different medium."

"Tell me more"

"Well, it is hard for me to explain. But I keep seeing you and Great-Grandpa in my dreams. And I know I'm supposed to do something, but I'm not sure what that is. But I'm sure that there is a higher purpose here, and it has something to do with space and time. I think I'm supposed to be a cosmic architect, or something like that, a position that doesn't exist today. I'm just not sure exactly what that is. Bottom line, I want to expand my major. I'm far enough along that I want to finish my architecture degree, but then I want to go to grad school for my PhD in theoretical physics."

She paused and looked expectantly at her father. "I hope you're not mad that I'm changing my mind ..."

"Mad? Why would I be mad? I only want you to be happy. And if this is what you want to do, then you will have my full support as always. I've always said you can do anything you put your mind to, and I mean that, little girl."

Maya grimaced at the reference. "Thanks, Daddy." She hesitated, "What should I tell Mom?"

"The truth, of course. This is exciting! And I want you to discuss your dreams with her as well."

Chapter 10

Dr. Kaminski stepped back from the lab table. He had been at it for ten straight hours and his back knew it. Science was a young man's game, and he wasn't young anymore. He thought briefly about his colleagues who were no longer with him. Wayne, Carl, others. He was the last of a generation, yet he still had important work to do.

Biology was never his strong suit, so he had consulted with others at Princeton. There was very little to go on in the field of theoretical biophysics. The questions he was asking about time-space rifts and genetic effects passed to later generations were theoretical at best. He tried to get answers, but most people weren't looking in the directions he wanted to go.

No matter, he had blazed trails before, and he would do so again. He looked at the chalkboard and made a few changes. Most professors used smart boards these days, but he still held out. Sometimes the old ways were better; or at least more comfortable.

The equation stared at him. His equation on time-space fracture. It had been over forty years since he first proposed it, and while he made some advancements towards proving it, it was largely still just a theory. One that very few people actually believed in.

But this was important. Future-of-the-universe important. He looked again at the logs that Cris had sent him. Logs for both him and his daughter, of both dreams and the larger "out of body" events. The data showed that the dreams had leveled off for the most part, averaging two per month. The larger events, however, had largely stopped.

He didn't know if that was good or bad, just that it was different. His theory didn't specifically predict either event, but it did allow for them. He knew there was something more there, something just beneath the surface, if he could only find it.

There had to be a variable that was unique to Wayne and his descendants. If he could find that, perhaps he could find the key. The key, if there was one, to solving this mystery.

In the years since he, Wayne, and Carl had participated in nuclear tests, the world had come down hard on the side of disarmament and nonnuclear weapons. As a result, there were no longer any opportunities to study the effects of such explosions. He only had his data from the last hydrogen bomb tests in the Marshall Islands so many years ago.

Maybe it wasn't in his DNA to figure this out. Maybe someone else would have to. DNA. DNA. There had to be something there. It must be the key, but to what and how he did not know.

He closed his eyes to think. He only hoped the answer would come to him soon enough. While he still had time on this earth. But that was not to be.

Chapter 11

W ayne and Carl drove down the dirt track through the desert. The moon cast long shadows across their path, occasionally interrupted by passing clouds. The area seemed completely deserted, which it was, seeing as radiation levels here were still much higher than normal.

Wayne braked to a halt. "This is as far as we can take the jeep. Any farther and we won't be able to decontaminate the metal."

Carl jumped down and checked his radiation suit. "All right! We're walking from here. Grab the collector; I've got the flashlight and Geiger counter."

The two continued on across the desolate landscape, like two lone explorers on the moon. Even after several years, nothing had been able to grow back within the immediate blast zone. And desert animals still stayed well clear; they could somehow sense this was a place of death and destruction. Carl's light illuminated a faint path in front of them as they trudged forward to ground zero.

After an hour, they made it to the blast crater. Over one-thousand feet across and ten feet deep. They lowered themselves down and made their way to the center. The ground here was smooth and glassy from the radiation and force of the explosion. The Geiger counter clacked furiously as they approached the center.

As they got closer, Wayne slowed and then stopped. "I can feel it, right here. This is where it happened."

Carl checked the instrument, "You're right, this is it. Exactly ground zero. What now?"

Wayne studied him for a moment. "I think I need to take off my suit"

"No! That will kill you. There is enough radiation here to kill any living thing on earth that wanders through here. Why would you do that?"

"Because I need to know. Remember what happened in the lab? With the rock sample? What if it happens here on a larger scale? I need to know!"

Before Carl could protest, Wayne reached up and pulled off the headgear of his suit. The air felt cool on his face, but odorless, sterile. As if there were no living thing within miles.

Carl checked the Geiger readings - it had stopped clicking. Just as in the lab. He waved it around Wayne and the immediate surroundings, and there was nothing. When he walked away out of Wayne's reach, the readings came back. There was a bubble around Wayne where no radiation was detected.

Carl looked at Wayne. "How do you feel? Can you sense anything different?"

"I feel fine, but I also feel somewhat disconnected. Like I am not fully here. Like...." Wayne suddenly went completely rigid. "Do you see them?" he asked Carl.

"Who? Where?"

"Right there!" Wayne pointed a few feet in front of them. "Standing there. Looking at us."

"No, I don't see anything. Are you sure?"

"Yes, I'm sure, and they look familiar, although I've never met them before. A man and a woman. They are reaching out to me ... and they just vanished." Wayne turned to Carl. "What do you think that means?"

"I don't know, but we shouldn't stay here to discuss it. We don't know yet if there are limits to your radiation tolerance, and I know that even with this suit on, I will have maxed out my exposure in another few minutes. No reason to tempt fate."

Wayne put his hood back on and they headed back the way they had come. The experiment had reproduced the results from the lab, but it didn't tell them much else.

"Wayne, we'll keep on trying. The South Pacific should help us, too."

Chapter 12

Wayne opened his eyes in the recovery room. His chest hurt, but that made sense when they cracked you open to put an artificial valve in your heart.

"Hey, Dad, how do you feel?" Eleanor looked down at him.

"Not bad, considering," he replied. He raised his hand and Eleanor took it. "Good to see you, dear"

"You too, Dad. They say the operation went very well. Textbook. We'll be able to bring you home in a few days. The kids have a surprise party planned for you."

"Good. Where's Mom, I'd like to see her."

"She's back at home. You can only have one visitor at a time, and we weren't sure how long you'd be."

"Send her my love, will you?" said Wayne. And he closed his eyes, let the drugs take over again, and drifted back to sleep.

The party was a smashing success. The grandkids had made welcome home banners that hung from the ceiling. There were balloons. And cake - both for

Grandpa's homecoming and his younger grandson's birthday.

Wayne enjoyed the whole thing very much. To be surrounded by the love of his family made him feel complete. This was another step in his recovery, one that he hoped to make soon so he could get back to work.

His wife and daughters didn't know he was working again. He used the excuses of his ham radios and oil paintings to escape to the basement for hours on end. But in that time, he was working on the time-space fracture problem. He knew he was somehow at the center of it, and he needed to solve it while he still had time before him.

He was feeling tired so he headed to bed. It was important that he get his rest. Everyone said goodnight to him. Cris hung back a moment and gave him an extra hug. "I love you, Grandpa"

"And me, you. Now let me sleep so I can be fresh in the morning. We'll discuss the elements if you're up for it."

"You bet! See you tomorrow, Grandpa!"

Later that night after everyone was asleep, Wayne was awakened by a sound near his bed. "Grandpa, wake up."

"Cristian, is that you? What time is it?"

"It's me, and I have someone for you to meet. Your great-granddaughter, Maya"

"My what? But...." Wayne sat up and looked to see his fully grown grandson standing there next to a woman in her early thirties.

"Maya, this is your great-grandpa Howell. Grandpa, this is your great-granddaughter, Maya."

"Pleased to meet you," said Maya, and gave him a hug.

"Me, too," replied Wayne as he hugged her back. "But why are you here? How are you here? The last I saw you was the singularity on Eniwetok with the Bravo device. What's happening?"

"Well, Great-Grandpa, to make a very long story short, I followed in your footsteps as a nuclear physicist. And I cracked the time-space fracture equation and how to use it to move through time, space, and other dimensions.

"The problem is that we are the only ones who can do it. Your DNA was altered that day at the Trinity site, and you passed that on to us. For some reason, it did not have the same effect on all of your descendants; we are the only three."

"But the bigger problem is that if we don't stop it, the rift will continue to grow. I have mapped it out forward and backward. It is like a giant spider's...."

"Web," said Wayne. "I've seen it before."

"Yes, a web" continued Maya. "One that is unraveling fast at the outer edges working back from our genealogical line. It is traveling upstream in time and space, and it will tear the universe apart if it is not stopped."

"So what do we do?" asked Wayne

"Well, here's the thing: I have architected a solution. A very elegant one if I do say so myself, but it is not complete. I need two things to finish it. Firstly, I need a nuclear physicist who understands this field almost as well as I do, and secondly, I need the person at the point of origin." She hesitated, "In other words, I need you."

"Okay. Let's get started. What do you need me to do?"

Maya looked at her father. Cris responded, "It's not that easy. We need you to go forward with Maya to her time. Permanently. The fix she is describing will only work if you are there. Unfortunately, the way the phenomenon works, you will not be able to access your body again in this time. You will have been gone too long. Your body will still exist in other times, and you will be able to jump among those, but this one will be forever cutoff. For everyone in this current time, you will have died. Since you will not be able to come back, in essence for everyone now, you will have died."

Wayne looked over to the other bed where Meredith lay sleeping. "I need to say goodbye."

Maya interjected "I'm sorry, but there is not enough time. The portal I used to get us here is closing in seconds - I need to get us back through now."

Cris grabbed Wayne's hand. "It's okay. I was here this day when you died. I still remember it clearly. And while we were all sad, we carried on. Grandma carried on. We made it because we had each other. But none of us will make it much longer if you don't do this."

Wayne nodded, "Okay." He looked one last time at his wife. "I love you, Maggie, forever." Tears slowly streamed down his face. He turned to Maya.

Maya nodded. "Look up and reach up - the universe will do the rest". As he did so, his soul escaped up through the portal and into another dimension and on into the future with Maya.

Chapter 13

"Great-Grandpa seems like too much to say all the time, don't you think? What if I call you GG Howell from now on?"

"You could call me Wayne, which is my name. You're fully grown at this point, it would be okay."

Maya smiled. "I know, but it still feels weird."

"No weirder than jumping sixty years into the future with your great-granddaughter?"

"Good point, GG Howell, good point. Okay, let's see what we have here."

The research was all laid out before them. "It appears that the Bravo event is the way to go - where we should look. It was the highest yield nuclear test of the time, so it gives us the best chance to put it all back together."

"I agree, Maya, but how do we do it in a way that ensures everything continues as it should?"

"I have a theory about that." Maya pulled up the time-space fracture equation on the screen. "This variable here represents the nominal effect of high-intensity radiation on the space-time continuum. If that could be neutralized, so there is no radiation effect, I think we can reverse the tear and end it there."

"I see, I see. Theoretically possible, of course. But how do we do that? Do you have technology now available that can do that?"

"No, but even if we did, we wouldn't be able to get it through the portal. We are the only ones that can transport. Anything larger than the clothes on our backs has never made it."

"But you do have an idea, don't you?" he asked with a sparkle in his eye.

"Yes, I do, and it involves you. I think you are the key to all of this. You are the anti-radiation source that we need. If you are at the point of singularity, then, in theory, you will absorb the radiation in that instant, and the rip that started at Trinity can be repaired. I think I know how to do that."

"So we'll have to sacrifice ourselves to make this happen?"

"I'm not as clear on that part. It is possible that two or three of us will survive."

"Three of us? How do you get three?"

"Dad has to come with us. I need you to absorb the radiation, me to fix the tear, and Dad to hold us together. I'm afraid we'll get out of sync if not directly connected. He is the only one who can do that."

"What about me in 1954? I'll be there?"

"Yes, you'll be there, and we'll need that version of you to initiate the chain reaction, but we can't use that version alone because if we did, we wouldn't be able to bring you forward at age seventy-seven the way we did. We would be stuck in an endless time loop. It has to be you, here before me, who does this."

"Okay, I understand. When do we make this happen?"

"Time is infinite and finite. It is a straight line and an endless loop. It is a paradox. So while we are heading back in time, and could do that from any other time, there is a very real time limit. I have calculated based on the time-space fracture equation, and we only have another few weeks before it is too late. Based on the available portals, we should target the day after tomorrow to do this."

"And I need to bring my father from when I was seven. That's when I first had alignment with the seven year old version of him. Also, he was forty-three then, and I don't think it's a coincidence that the sum our ages, forty-three and thirty-four, equals your age of seventy-seven. It has to be then. I can send word through my younger self so he is ready."

"You can do that?"

"I have been experimenting for the last several years, and I have learned how to move forward and backward within myself. I suspect I am the only one of us who can do that because I am three generations removed from the original rift. This has allowed my genetic material to deviate enough to allow this. For you and my dad, the divergence is too small."

"One question you have never answered: why doesn't Eleanor have the genetic deviation that was passed to your father and then to you?"

"I've thought about that quite a bit, and unfortunately, I don't have an answer. That troubles me, because according to everything else I've seen, she definitely should have. The fact that she does not means that there is another variable that I have missed. I don't know how critical that is to what we are going to attempt, but it is something we need to keep an eye on. We may have to adjust on the fly."

"Well, I'm ready when you are. I'm glad I got to know you, Great-Granddaughter."

"And me, you, Great-Grandpa. Now I understand why my dad loved you so much."

Chapter 14

"**D**addy, Daddy!" Maya burst into the room. "I had another dream!"

"You did?" Cris responded with half-opened eyes. "What was this one about?"

"This one was about me when I'm older. Thirty-four! That's so old!"

"Hey, it's not that old!" Cris grinned. "So what happened in this dream?"

"Well, I was a scientist and I came back to get you so we could travel together, like the time when we went to see Great-Grandpa. Do you remember that?"

Cris was awake now. He sat up and looked at Jennifer. To Maya, he asked, "When does this dream take place?"

"Tomorrow, Daddy, tomorrow!" And with that, Maya leapt up, gave each of her parents a kiss, and ran from the room.

Cris looked at his wife again. "Tomorrow."

"What if you don't come back this time? What do I do with Maya?"

"Take care of her. Help her grow. Help her understand that her daddy did what he had to for her and for everyone's future. I can't promise I'll be back, but from what I understand, if I don't do this, none of us will be around much longer."

He took Jennifer in his arms and held her tight. Letting their heartbeats become one as they lay there together, each contemplating what tomorrow would bring.

"I love you."

"I love you, too."

The sun rose bright and clear the next morning. Cris was up early. He didn't know when the time would come, but he wanted to be ready. He kissed his girls, one each on their foreheads, and went downstairs to prepare himself.

When he got there, his thirty-four-year-old daughter and seventy-seven-year-old grandfather were waiting for him. "Good morning, Maya, Grandpa."

They exchanged hugs and pleasantries, and then Maya went over the plan.

They would be jumping into Eniwetok just moments before detonation. Wayne would need to be close enough to the device to step into the singularity when it was first created. As he did that, Maya would use her skills and training to "mend" the rift. She couldn't really explain how she would do that, but she knew what to do based on her years of research.

Cris's job was to keep the three of them together. With the forces at play, they could easily become separated without direct contact. He was to be that contact.

They wrapped up and prepared to leave. Just then, seven-year-old Maya ran into the room. "Daddy, who are these people? She looks familiar. Him, too."

Cris smiled at his little girl with a knowing glance at the grown version. "I'll tell you when you're older. You wouldn't believe me anyway."

"When I'm how old? I want to know now! How about when I'm eight? Or nine?"

Adult Maya looked down and said, "He'll tell you when you are twenty-one. It will be when you are home for Thanksgiving break your junior year of college. You can go write that down in a place where you'll never lose it."

"Okay!" And little Maya bounded from the room to go write it down. And in the space provided, the three family members joined hands, locked eyes, and Maya transported them back in time. Back to the second hydrogen bomb test on Eniwetok. Back to save the future of the universe.

Chapter 15

Wayne looked at the display in the bunker. "All systems are nominal, we're looking good!" He turned to Carl and Norm. "I'm glad you two are here."

Norm responded: "I wouldn't have it any other way. Mind if I stand right next to you at the time of the detonation? I want to be sure that I can closely monitor you."

Wayne nodded affirmation as he continued fine-tuning the instruments. Carl was doing the same two stations away. This test was to be even larger than Mike - by a scale of two to one. Whatever was left of the atoll would be gone after this.

As with before, the countdown started over the loudspeaker.

"10 ... 9 ... 8..."

Norm leaned into Wayne. "It will be all right."

"I hope so"

"6 ... 5 ... 4..."

"It will be, my friend."

"2 ... 1..."

And as light began to explode before his eyes, Wayne could feel Norm's comforting presence beside him, watching him as he jumped to the singularity.

The first to arrive were the trio from the future – Wayne, age seventy-seven, Maya age thirty-four, and Cris, age forty-three. They immediately took up positions around the device, hand-in-hand, ready for the singularity.

At the point of detonation, the singularity formed, and the elder Wayne stepped in to absorb the radiation. He took the full blast and began to turn inward. It was too much at once, too much energy, too much power to control. But he must, he knew he must, so he held on, tenuously.

Maya looked for the rift. She could see it extending out from Wayne through Cris, through her, and back. She saw it extending back to the younger Wayne, from this time, who had now arrived.

"This is the decisive moment!" she shouted above the din. The cosmic symphony crashed and boomed all around her. Power leaking from the elder Wayne flowed around her, knocking her off balance. Cris grabbed her tightly and held her with his mind.

I have you, dear, he thought to her. *And you, too, Grandfather*, he thought to the elder Wayne.

To the younger Wayne, Maya called, "Help your older self! He can't absorb all the radiation alone. There is still too much for me to heal the tear!"

The younger Wayne moved toward his elder self and began sharing the radiation. But it was not working as intended. Rather than increasing the amount of absorption, it was spreading it out evenly across the two of them – but with opposite polarity, which was actually pushing each of them further apart. It was an uphill battle that neither man was winning.

Maya stepped in. "This isn't working. At this rate, I won't have time to repair the rift. We need to find a different way.

"Great-Grandpa, I have to send you back. I suddenly understand that this must be done by three, always by three. The three of us, we are the trinity, the trinity that connects this and binds this and explains this.

"We are the trinity that must see this through, and while it can be the various forms of us from time to time, we cannot use multiple versions of ourselves to form the trinity. It must always be one of each of us: grandfather, grandson, and great-granddaughter."

Tears streamed down her face, "Thank you, and I love you, but I must now send you back." She closed her eyes, and at that moment, the younger Wayne was suddenly jerked back.

A scream escaped his lips, "No!" But he knew there was nothing he could do. It was now out of his hands.

Norm grabbed hold of him, "What happened? Were you successful?"

Wayne pulled back and looked at his friend, his colleague. "I don't know, they were not able to keep me there with them. They are still trying, but I can't help." He looked down dejectedly. "I can't help."

"No, you're wrong!" Norm shook Wayne. "I've played with my theory for twenty years and I know that you are the only one who can truly fix this. In the end it will be you, even if it is not today. I know that!"

"But what about them?" Wayne turned to the monitors. The nuclear reaction was in full bloom now, and the singularity was expanding into the nuclear explosion. "Will they be able to survive? They came to stop this madness, not perish in it!"

In anguish, Wayne watched the distant fireball grow from the explosion. He put his head in his hands and wept. Wept for the three he had lost. Wept for the future that was now gone. Wept for his friend who tried to comfort him.

"What have I done?" he cried.

In the singularity, the three of them were suddenly alone. Time stopped ever so briefly as they struggled against the forces around them - the naked singularity and the ever-expanding gap in the cosmic web.

"I can't hold it together!" Maya shouted. "It's widening!"

"I can't hold the energy any longer," Wayne cried, "It is getting away from me!"

And in a pure moment of clarity, Cris saw everything. He saw his past, his future, his present all as one. He saw his ancestors, he saw his descendants. He saw an unbroken chain through the millennia that went right through him.

He understood why his mother had not shown this talent. She had been conceived prior to the Trinity test. Grandpa had not had the opportunity to pass on the rift through his genes. But that did not explain how Cris had acquired it, why he and his daughter Maya had this genetic connection. That was still unclear. He could not explain that. But what was also clear was that Cris was the inflection point. The connection between them all. Grandpa might be the original source of the defect, and Maya might be the most adept at using it, but Cris was the connection. Cris at age seven when his grandfather died. Cris at age forty-three when Maya age seven experienced the shared dream. He saw the unbroken line, and he felt love.

Love that expanded outwards in all directions. That called to him across the ages. That followed the spider web of time and space that connected all beings across all dimensions. He saw the rift at their center that they were trying to heal. And he knew that he could heal it by stepping into it.

He turned to his grandfather, and then his daughter. To each, he simply said, "I love you." Tears of joy rolled down his face as he prepared to take the next step. He turned once more to Maya, "I will find you. Somehow, someway, I will find you."

"Daddy, no! Don't do this. Don't leave me!"

"I must."

"Then I will find you, too. No matter how long it takes, I will find you."

And then he stepped into the rift.

Time, space, light, matter, energy expanded in all directions around him. He became one with the universe. He wept at the size and beauty of it all around him. He embraced his family, all families, with his ever-expanding consciousness. He felt like he was doing what he was meant to do for the very first time in his life.

Using both hands, he gripped the sides of the rift and pulled them close together. He used his love to seal it, one inch at a time. It took years, decades, centuries for him to do this, but in this space-time, it also happened immediately. It was both infinite and finite together.

His grandfather was absorbed by the singularity and vanished into another dimension. His time had come, and he was willing to make that sacrifice. There was nothing that Cris could do about that.

Maya was thrown back into the future. Back to where she had started. Dr. Manning, age thirty-four, in her lab.

Cris was absorbed by the rift and then expelled back into time and space. Adrift, alone, disoriented, but the rift was sealed. There he floated for a time before he was sucked back into the timeline. But not where he had started, rather back to the summer of 1945, before the Trinity test. Before this had all started. Back where he could stop it from happening again.

Chapter 16

Maya opened her eyes. The lab was dark. The only illumination came from the EXIT sign over the door. She shook her head and her senses slowly came back to her. She wasn't sure what had just happened.

Then it all came crashing back to her. "Dad!" she shouted in nothingness. She grabbed her phone to call her parents. "Mom, Mom, is Daddy there? Can I speak with him?"

There was a pause, and Maya heard her mom breathing on the phone. "No, dear, he's not here. Remember, he never came back that day he left when you were seven. We haven't seen him in over twenty-five years."

"No, nooooooo!" Maya sobbed into her hands. "I just saw him. I was just with him from that day. He never came back?"

"No, dear, he never did." Another long pause ensued. "Why don't you come up this weekend and I'll tell you about him? I always did like telling you about him."

"Mom, I'll do that, but this time I'll tell you about him. About my dad and how he saved everything – everyone."

Chapter 17

C ris opened his eyes. He was lying on the ground, in the desert. It was early morning or late evening - he wasn't sure. A few clouds scudded overhead.

He sat up and saw equipment everywhere. A large structure was being built. He could see the skeleton rising several stories into the air. From it hung a pulley system connected to a large, metal object.

As he began to stand, a voice called out, "You, stop! Show me your hands!"

He turned to see an Army MP with rifle drawn approach him. "Who are you, Sir? What are you doing here?"

Cris looked down and around and then back to the MP. "I don't know. Where am I?"

"You are in the New Mexico desert, near Los Alamos. And I have to take you into custody as part of national security." Rough hands grabbed Cris by the shoulders and wrestled him to the ground. He was handcuffed and dragged to a waiting jeep. Before they drove away, he heard a man ask about all the commotion.

The guard replied, "Nothing, Dr. Howell, just some guy who wandered onto the range. We're taking him in for questioning."

Cris turned to look for his grandfather, but the jeep was already bouncing away. As it turned down the dirt road, he saw the Gadget being hoisted up and being prepared for the first atomic test.

The jeep pulled into a stockade and Cris was escorted into the building and a waiting, empty cell. He sat there thinking, trying to wrap his brain around what had happened. Here he was, apparently back in time prior to the first Trinity test. He was not sure yet what this meant, but he knew he had to speak with his grandfather.

An Army captain walked in and broke his reverie. The man was young, tough-looking. He sat down across from Cris and gave him a look that was meant to intimidate him, but Cris just returned the stare. There was nothing this man could say or do that compared in any way to what he had just experienced.

The captain spoke first, "You are in a lot of trouble. Found inside a secure military installation during a time of war? You could be looking at life in prison. Or worse, execution if you are a spy. But if you are open now, that can have a big effect on the outcome."

Cris smiled, "I have nothing to hide. What is it you would like to know?"

"You had no identification on you. What is your name?"

"Cristian. Cristian Howell. I'm related to Dr. Wayne Howell."

"Oh, you are, are you? That will be easy enough to confirm. What were you doing out there on the range? That is a restricted area."

"You wouldn't believe me if I told you." Cris scratched his nose. "What basis do you have for holding me?"

"Under the Army War Powers Act of 1942, you are charged with trespassing on a secure military installation. Under the auspices of national security, I am detaining you. You say I won't believe you? Well, try me."

"You really won't believe me. I don't think I should say anything more at this time. I wonder if this has something to do with how it all started...." Cris trailed off as his mind raced to consider the possibilities.

The captain pressed again, "What was that? When what started?"

"Oh, nothing. I want to speak with my gran ... I mean my relative. Dr. Howell".

The captain leaned back and sighed. He could see that he was not going to get anything else out of this man at this time. "I'll see what I can do. In the meantime, get comfortable, you may be here for a very long time."

The captain left the cell and Cris was left to his thoughts. His memory was clearing, and he was piecing together what had happened. He remembered being on Eniwetok and trying to repair the rift with his grandfather and daughter. He remembered the younger version of his grandfather appearing, and that his two grandfathers together had inadvertently worked against them. How Maya was not able to repair the rift as she had planned. And then how he had stepped in the rift to repair it, sacrificing his former life and essentially his daughter's, too.

He laid his head in his hands. Was it worth it? If Maya was correct and it saved the universe, then rationally he had to say yes, although at the moment he was in too much emotional turmoil to admit that. He wouldn't get to see his daughter grow up. *His daughter would grow up without a father.* The thought gnawed at him, and large, hot tears slowly streamed down his face.

There had to be a way to get back. There had to be! He loved his family too much not to try everything he could to do that. Maybe his grandfather could help. There had to be something he could do!

Maya sat in the living room of her parent's home. *No, Mother's home*, she mentally corrected herself. Everything was as she remembered it, except there were very few remnants of her father. Nothing of the man she remembered taking her to soccer practice, or to swimming lessons, or to look for colleges. The absence of him was a physical thing, overwhelming.

Her mother walked in with a tray loaded with tea and biscuits. At least some things never changed. Jennifer poured a cup for each of them and sat down. Maya held hers to her lips and blew on it as it warmed her hands. She took a sip and said, "I saw him yesterday. On Eniwetok. Trying to fix the rift."

Jennifer looked at her. "I don't know what to say, dear. He's been gone for almost three decades. He's not coming back at this point."

"I can't accept that. He's my father, he wouldn't leave me."

"I'm sure if there were a way, he would have found it by now. I am sure of that. But he did what he had to do, I guess. Although that doesn't make it any easier." Jennifer took a long sip. "I've never stopped missing him, but I moved on."

"Here, let me show you some of his old photos, like we used to." Her mom took a couple of photo albums down off the shelf. "Which one do you want to start with?"

"Your wedding, of course" Maya said with a smile. They always started with the wedding. As they turned the pages, Maya could see the love that her parents had shared. They looked so happy. So young. So full of life. A life they started together that led to her, and one that she had unwittingly torn apart.

"Mom, I'm sorry. This is my fault. This wouldn't have happened if I hadn't brought him with us." Maya began to sob in her mom's arms. "I'm so sorry."

"There, there, dear. One thing your father always said was that we make our own choices. He didn't have to go - he chose to go. It is not your fault.

"Eniwetok, you say? Here is the album from his grandparents. You never knew them - they had both passed away before you were born."

Maya looked at her and smiled. "Sure, let's look at that one; you can point them out to me." She sat closer as her mother turned the pages.

"This actually starts at Los Alamos. Apparently, your great-grandpa Howell was involved in the Manhattan Project. There should be a picture of him in here somewhere - oh, there it is. That's him standing in front of the first atomic bomb. They called it 'The Gadget,' I believe. Your dad was always so proud of his grandpa."

But Maya didn't hear that last part. She was too busy staring at the jeep in the side of the picture. The one with her father sitting in the back looking toward his grandfather as it pulled away.

Later that evening, Maya lay awake in her old bed, staring at the stars she had pasted to the ceiling. She had made sure all the major constellations were represented, to scale no less, and she would lie awake for hours practicing their names. It was the best she could do living in Philadelphia. They were lucky if they could see the Big Dipper on a clear day with all the city lights.

She lay there considering her options. It appeared that Dad had sealed the rift. The readings she could pick up confirmed that was the case. Surprisingly, the vibration in her DNA was still present, so it was possible that she could still bounce through time. What that meant, she was not sure, but in her experience, she was only able to do that around the time of a nuclear event.

Of course, that picture had to be taken prior to the detonation of the first device, so it should be possible for her to travel back to the singularity, but what good would that do if her father was not there as well? He could be anywhere at that time, and he had not learned to jump on his own - only with her assistance.

So many options, yet none appeared to be very viable. She thought about GG Howell. She missed him, too, although in a different way. She had only met him as an adult and so did not have the same level of connection as she did with her dad.

This was going to become the focus of her research from here on out – how to go back and get her dad, even if it meant she died in the attempt. She owed that to him. And she owed that to her younger self.

As she drifted off to sleep, her last thought was of her dad kissing her goodnight.

Chapter 18

C ris was awakened in his cell the next morning by the sound of the duty change. He was given a light breakfast, and then the captain was back for more.

"I checked with Dr. Howell, and he has no relatives named Cristian. Nice try, but I'll ask again. What is your name?"

"Give me a lie detector test - I will prove my name is Cristian."

"Lie detector test? What's that? How can a test tell if you are lying?"

"Never mind. Look, I really need to speak with Dr. Howell. This is an urgent matter."

"Not going to happen," answered the captain. "No one gets in or out of here unless I say so, and I say no."

Cris had anticipated that reaction, so he tried a different tact. "Look, I sabotaged the device when I was out there, before your boys picked me up. It is so subtle that I doubt anybody will be able to find it. I guarantee it won't work, unless I speak with Dr. Howell. If I'm allowed to, I will share what I did with the device."

The captain stared at him speechlessly for a moment. "Are you saying that you know what that device is?"

"Not only do I know what it is, but I also know how to stop it from ever working. Unless I get to speak with Dr. Howell. I'm not saying another word until you let me."

The captain stood to leave. "I'll speak with my superiors about this."

An hour later, the captain returned with a young scientist in tow. "Dr. Howell, this is the prisoner I told you about. The one who says he is related to you."

"Does he now," replied Wayne. "Well, let's see who we have here." He stepped closer to the bars. "So how is it that we are related?"

Cris stood up, "Very distantly, Sir, very distantly. I'd be happy to explain, but I'd rather do so in private."

The captain stepped in, "No way. That is not happening. I will not leave one of our senior scientists alone with a saboteur."

Wayne looked at the captain, "Oh, come now, Captain. He is behind bars, is he not? And you have searched to be sure he has no weapons? No, I'll be perfectly fine. Let me see what he has to say, and I can pass on anything of relevance to you."

The captain was not pleased, but he deferred. "I'll be just outside, Dr. Howell, if you require anything." With a huff, he turned and walked out of the room.

"So, what do you have to say for yourself ... Cristian, is it?"

"That's right, Cristian, just as your middle name."

Wayne smiled, "That doesn't mean anything. My middle name is public knowledge around here."

"I'm sure that is true. But spelled without the 'h'? The way my name is spelled?" he paused to let that sink in. "Look, I have a fantastic story to tell you. One that I doubt you will believe. One that I would not believe if I were in your shoes. I don't know where to start."

"Well," replied Wayne, "in my experience, the beginning is always a good place."

So Cris did start from the beginning. From the beginning of everything. The whole fantastic tale, start to finish. When he was done, Wayne leaned back in his chair and lit his pipe. "So you are saying you are my grandson?"

"That's right, from your daughter, Eleanor, who has yet to be born."

"And the nuclear test we are conducting in a few days somehow set this whole chain in motion?"

"That's right. I haven't sabotaged the device; I only said that to gain access to you. My primary purpose is to find my way home, to my daughter."

"In the future?"

"Yes, in the future. You are the only one I could think of to help me."

"And tell me one more time, where was I born and how did I meet your ... grandmother?"

"I don't know the city for sure. I want to say Osage. But I know that it was in Kansas and that you met on the train to the University of Kansas where you were both studying. Grandma always said how unusual it was for a woman to study physics back then."

"That it was, and still is. So what would you propose we do with you?"

"Well, that is the question. If I know my daughter, she is trying to find a way to get me back, but I don't think she can do it alone. I think she will need my help, and possibly yours, too."

Wayne paused for a moment, and then called in the captain. "Captain, as always you and your men have done a fine job with security. Cristian here has just given me a full debrief of his capture and questioning. He was planted to test your measures with an outside source, and I must say they were exemplary. Now, if you would be so good as to release my cousin, we'll be on our way."

"Your cousin? He's your cousin?"

"That's right, Captain. Now let's go, time is a wasting."

That evening after dinner, Wayne and Cris sat down outside the single barracks.

"Maggie wasn't allowed to come with me this time. Security is too tight. I do miss her, especially after the stillbirth."

Cris looked at his grandfather, "Andrew."

"Yes, Andrew. That is the part of your story I found most believable. No one else knows that we named him - they only know that we lost the baby." Wayne looked to the stars. "But it appears that we will be successful our next time out, and that it will lead to you." Wayne clapped Cris on the back. "How about that!"

Cris smiled. "Yes, how about that. Now if we could only find a way to get me back home...."

"About that, I've been thinking. You said there was some kind of a disturbance at the first atomic test, correct?" Cris nodded. "Well, many physicists believe time is a loop, so I have a theory, but before I get to that, tell me again about how you transported in the past."

Cris looked up at the stars as he spoke. "In each instance, it was with my daughter, Maya, and the hops were always centered on a nuclear event. The only one that wasn't was the one when you ... actually, I probably shouldn't tell you about that one."

Wayne looked over at Cris. "Something I may not like?"

"Well, let's just say that is one you should not see coming. You'll understand when the time comes. But, yes, the other two were tied to hydrogen bomb tests in the South Pacific."

Wayne smiled, "So that means, of course, that this thing will work, right? There are a number of us around here who are not so sure. This is the first time we are trying something like this, after all."

"Oh, it will work all right." Cris shook his head. "It will work better than you can possibly imagine. But back to your theory, what is it?"

"Well, see if you can follow this. Firstly, you said your prior jumps, with one exception, have all centered on nuclear events, correct?" Cris nodded his agreement. "And you said that if you know your daughter, she will stop at nothing to come find you, right?"

"Right."

"And you stated that at the first test, there was some kind of anomaly that set this whole string in motion, right?"

"Yes, that's also right."

"Okay, so back to the concept of time as a circle. It is postulated that if you keep going around the circle of time, eventually all events will happen again. Or said another way, time doesn't really change, it just circles around again. Got it?"

"Yes, I think so."

"All right, so what if this event has already happened before, and what if it is destined to happen again? It already has for you, right? Well, what if the anomaly for the first test was YOU at ground zero. And your daughter was there to pick you up and take you forward in time?"

The light slowly began to dawn for Cris. "So you're saying that everything that has happened in your future has happened in my past, and is destined to happen again. Including me being at ground zero for the first atomic test, setting this whole thing in motion?"

"That's right. And I have one more detail to add to the theory. Remember when you told me the whole story that you couldn't explain why your mother and siblings didn't show any of the symptoms that you did?"

"Yes, what about that?"

"Well, here is a little known secret. Maggie is already pregnant. And if you are right, that will be your mother, Eleanor. So she does not have the genetic defect that you and I will have. The defect that you and I could have acquired by being at the first atomic test."

The implications of that sunk in. "So that which I journeyed to stop, I also created?"

"Very possibly, yes. The question, then, I think, is how to prevent it from happening this time around. And we only have two days to figure that out before the test."

Chapter 19

Maya finished breakfast with her mother. "Mom, I've made a decision. I'm going back to find Dad."

Jennifer looked down in her tea and a wry smile formed on her face. "Somehow I knew you were going to say that. You are a lot like him, you know."

"I know. And before you say it – yes, I'll be careful. Of course, if I'm successful, you won't know it because your life will be how I remember it."

"And if you're not successful? What then?"

"You'll know that I did everything I could to save my father, and that if I don't come back, I love you and him very much."

They embraced at that point, possibly for the final time, and Maya headed back to D.C. and her lab.

Later that night, Maya rested her head on the lab table. She had been at it for several hours without rest, reworking the equations again and again. There were two complicating facts. The first was she wasn't sure if her father would even be there. If he didn't figure it out, then the rest didn't matter.

The second was if he were there, then the rest mattered. It mattered a lot. And she hadn't figured out that part of it yet. She had always traveled before with the three of them connected in some way. This time, she was looking at traveling in a pair, and it looked like, according to theory, that may be what had started the rift in the first place.

For some reason, the equation always worked out to the number three, no matter what she did. As if that were some divine number or sequence. Always in threes. And that was ultimately the problem. Should she risk it as two, hoping her theory could be wrong and they would be fine? Or forego it because to do so would cause the very rift they were trying to stop?

But there was another possibility. One that she had learned from her father: always fight to live another day. Even if she was right, and they formed the rift in this attempt, wouldn't it be worth it to get him back and do it all over again? They had succeeded, in a way, once, so why not again?

That was an awfully big gamble to take with the fate of the universe in one's hands, but then sometimes the answer isn't always logical. Sometimes the answer is Love. And that is what was driving Maya.

She shook herself back to focus. Okay. There was a lot to do to prepare for her jump, not the least of which was that she needed to get some sleep. She had to be alert tomorrow for the big day.

She hit the lights and headed for the door.

Chapter 20

C ris and Wayne were eating breakfast the morning of the test.

"Grandpa?"

"I'm still not used to you calling me that," Wayne said with a smile.

"It feels weird for me, too, especially because at the moment, I'm older than you!" They both chuckled. "Listen, I have a request of you. It may seem unusual, but it is important. After the test, can you find a piece of Trinitite...?"

"Trinitite?"

"Yes, Trinitite. That's what they will call the radioactive glass formed by the explosion. Can you find a piece and mail it to your great-granddaughter? I will give you the address, and you'll have to ask the postal service to deliver it in the future. They will think you are crazy, but trust me, this is important."

"Sure, I can do that for you. Is there anything else?"

"No, just be sure that Eleanor gives me the same name!"

"That I can do. Now let's get back to the plan for this evening."

Wayne went over every last detail one more time. And then it was time to go.

Cris hopped in the back of one of the covered jeeps, and Wayne drove it out to the test site. There were multiple checkpoints leading to the site, and with each, his badge easily got him through. Until the last one.

"I'm sorry, Dr. Howell, but I don't have you on the list for clearance today." The MP was respectful, but firm. "I need to ask you to turn around."

"I can appreciate your situation, Sergeant, but if I don't perform one last check of the firing mechanism, it is possible that this test will be a nonevent. I would hate for that to be the case."

"But, Sir, my orders are very clear. No one is to have access unless they are on the list."

"How about a compromise? What if you come with me and follow my movements? I don't have to open the device - a visual inspection to be sure the leads are all in place will do."

The MP shifted nervously from one leg to another. "Let me call my captain and check in." He stepped back from the jeep and pulled out his radio to call base. Wayne could see him shifting back and forth as he conversed with his superior. When he came back, he jumped in the passenger seat. "Okay. You have 15 minutes. And you are not to leave my sight at any time."

"No problem, Sergeant, this should take only five."

Wayne pulled through the gate and drove up and around the device. On the back side, he came to a stop and reached back to grab a toolkit. "Just in case," he said. "Let's go"

The two of them walked up to the frame where the bomb was suspended 100 feet in the air. Wayne looked up and traced the wiring from the bomb, along the frame, and down to the generator and remote detonation panel. He walked over to the panel and visually inspected it.

He turned to the MP. "This all looks good, Sergeant, let's head back. And thank you again."

They headed back to the jeep and drove back to the checkpoint. The MP stepped out and Wayne drove back to the command bunker where he would be situated for the test.

Cris knelt in the shadow of one of the generators as Wayne drove off. He knew he would have 20 minutes or so before all personnel were told to clear off. He bided his time thinking about his daughter. He had faith in her. He had to in order to be following this course of events, because if she didn't come, it would be suicide.

After what seemed an eternity, the evacuation broadcast came over the loudspeakers. "Attention, attention, this is the final warning. Repeat, final warning. All personnel are to evacuate back to their observation stations. This includes all forward personnel. This is your last warning. Countdown commences in 15 minutes."

The two MPs at the checkpoint jumped in their jeeps and headed down the road. Cris was now alone with the first atomic bomb. Waiting. For it to go off.

An odd stillness filled the air. He could see in all directions, which meant that he could be seen as well. He stayed low, behind the generator. The last thing he needed now was for someone to spy him and call off the test.

Cris was not religious by nature, but he thought this a good time to pray. He knelt and opened his heart to the heavens. "God, I know I haven't always been there for you, or even believed in you for that matter, but in case you are up there, I just want to say that I believe in the power of love. I have faith in my daughter. In my grandfather. And I believe based on all that I have seen in the last several weeks that if there is not a grand architect such as yourself, there ought to be. If for no other reason than to take credit for the beauty that is the universe. I have seen it all around me, and to this point I have largely taken it for granted. But no more. I have enjoyed this miracle of life until now, and I hope to go on enjoying it, but if now is my end, then I say thank you. Amen."

Cris crossed himself as the final countdown began. "Attention, attention, this commences the final countdown for Trinity test. All personnel, put on your protective gear, including goggles. Repeat, this is the final countdown and is not a drill."

"10 ... 9 ... 8 ... 7 ..."

Cris stood up and moved in under the device. This was it. If Maya was coming for him, it would be now.

"6 ... 5 ... 4 ... 3 ..."

In the command bunker, Wayne looked through his binoculars at the distant site. It was hard to see through his safety goggles. He thought he saw a shape under the device, but he couldn't be sure.

He stepped back and checked his instruments one last time. All systems were go. This was it. Either the dawn of the atomic age, or another failure. Whether permanent or not would remain to be seen.

But he had faith, had always had it, and he knew they had built a good device. And if Cristian, his grandson, were right, this would be a successful test.

He paused as the countdown approached zero. Carl, next to him, suddenly exclaimed, "I think there is someone out there!"

But it was too late, the countdown hit zero, and the sun was released on the surface of the earth.

Cris heard the countdown hit zero and closed his eyes. The next sound he heard was Maya in his ear, "Daddy, I'm here."

He turned to look, and there she was before him. Just as she had been that day on Eniwetok. "I knew you'd come," he said.

"And I knew you would be here," she replied.

In that instant, the device was triggered and the singularity created. Maya and Cris, daughter and father, stood in the center of it, were enveloped in it. But something was wrong.

"It's the rift!" Maya cried. "We are unstable because we are only two, not three!"

Cris yelled over the roar of the universe. "This has happened before, we have been here already. There has to be a way to stop it this time."

"Maybe there is," said a new voice. Both turned to see Wayne standing there – not Wayne from this time, but Wayne from the future. "After Eniwetok, I didn't go straight to the next dimension; I made a detour to here, to now, because I knew that you would need me."

Wayne stepped forward and embraced his grandson and his great-granddaughter. "This is my final step before I move on, but it should be enough for the two of you to return home, the fabric of space and time intact. We are the trinity at Trinity. We are in balance. Ages thirty-four, forty-three, and seventy-seven. It had to be this version of each of us together to do this. This version of each of us can be made in any combination of the other two of us – thirty-four, forty-three, and seventy-seven."

The three of them embraced one last time, and then shot forward in time as the first atomic fire raced out across the desert sands of New Mexico.

Chapter 21

A small team entered the site the next day. The destruction was ominous. The crater stretched over a thousand feet across and ten feet deep. Sand and rock all around had been turned to a green, radioactive glass.

Wayne was one of the scientists on this trip. He made sure when no one was looking to grab a piece of the glass that would later be known as Trinitite.

That night, he placed it in a lead-lined box with a note that stated, "It all started here, and you'll find that your DNA is the key," and wrapped it in a postal box with heavy brown paper. He addressed it to Maya Manning, with no return address. The postmaster in Santa Fe looked at him with a funny expression when he explained that he did not want the package delivered for nearly one-hundred years, but in the end, he relented. It certainly wasn't the strangest postal request he had ever received.

On the drive back to Los Alamos, Wayne reflected that he had no real way of knowing if Cristian and Maya had survived. It was possible that one or both was destroyed in the nuclear fire, in which case he didn't know what that would mean to the future. But of one thing he was sure: he had faith. Faith that they had made it. And faith that he would see them again someday. As their grandfather and great-grandfather when they were born.

Chapter 22

C ris walked in the front door of his house.

"Daddy! Daddy's home, Daddy's home!" Maya came tearing down the stairs and jumped into his arms for a huge hug.

"How long have I been gone?" he asked.

"Only a day, but I missed you. I can miss you, can't I?"

"You sure can, my dear, and guess what? I missed you, too, very much."

Jennifer came down the stairs. "So, how did it go?"

"You will never believe it. I'll tell you the whole thing, but you'll never believe it." Cris grinned and looked down at his daughter. "Suffice it to say, we have a very special girl. Very special. I wouldn't be here if it were not for her." He tousled her hair. "I love you both very much."

"And we both love you, Daddy," they said in unison as they all stepped in to a family hug.

Later that night, after Cris had told Jennifer the whole story, she held him tightly and softly wept. "So I almost lost you," she said in a whisper.

He leaned in and gave her a soft kiss on the top of her head. "You can't get rid of me that easily. No way." And he laid down his head to sleep.

That night, he had another dream. One with his grandfather from 1945, and one with his daughter of the future. They shared the same dream. And they knew that everything had turned out the way it was supposed to.

Chapter 23

C ris and Maya pulled into the driveway. Jennifer came out of the house and gave her daughter a huge hug. "It's good to see you again, dear. Welcome home for Thanksgiving."

"Thanks, Mom, it's good to be home."

That night over dinner, they discussed what Cris and Maya had talked about in the coffee shop earlier that day. Jennifer was onboard just the same as Cris. If that's what Maya really wanted, they would support her. Now and forever.

That night before bed, Maya came by her parents' room. "I just found a note I wrote to myself thirteen years ago. It says open at Thanksgiving during your junior year of college. That's now, so here goes."

She opened it, and inside it said, "Remember to ask Daddy who the people were in the kitchen that day when I was seven." Maya smiled and looked up, "I had completely forgotten about that! As I recall, you said something to the effect of 'You'll never believe it,' isn't that right?"

"Yes, that's what I said that day. So I'll tell you, but you won't believe it."

"Try me," Maya said as she sat at the end of the bed.

"Well...," Cris looked at his wife and then back to Maya, "that was your future self and your great-grandpa Howell." He paused to see her reaction.

"Seriously, Daddy, if you're not going to tell me, then just tell me you're not going to tell me. Don't make up something stupid like that." She jumped up. "I mean really, Daddy, you expect me to believe that?"

Cris smiled. "Believe what you want to, but you asked and I answered. I for one am now going to bed!"

Maya gave her parents each a quick peck and then bounded back to her room.

Cris and Jennifer smiled at each other and went to bed.

Chapter 24

Maya came up and entered the house. "Mom, Dad?" she called.

"In here" came her mom's voice from the kitchen. She nervously entered the room to see her mom sitting there having tea. Her heart dropped. Maybe he didn't make it back after all.

Just then, the back door opened, and in walked her father. "Daddy!" she cried, and ran and hugged him as fiercely as she had when she was a little girl. "I'm so glad to see you!"

Jennifer looked up, "What, no love for your mother? I birthed you, you know."

Maya grinned sheepishly. "It's not that. It's just that, well, I just got back from a trip and I just really missed Dad."

She looked to him and he looked deeply into her eyes. "You just got back?" he asked.

"Yes," she nodded.

"Well, you did it. I'm here; I've been here for the last twenty-seven years. And I have you to thank for that. I knew you'd come for me."

"And I knew you would be waiting for me as well."

"I love you, Daddy, Mommy."

"We love you, too," they responded in unison, and all stepped in for a family hug.

Later that night, Maya lay awake staring at her starry ceiling. The last time she had been here, the universe was out of whack and her dad was missing in time. Now he was back, and all was right again.

Her mind started to wander. Down all the cosmic places she had been. Along all the research she had completed. It seemed to her that something was missing.

She padded down the steps and sat down in the kitchen. She made herself a cup of tea and then headed outside to look at the stars. Space. Time. It all interconnected in a spider's web. A web she had crawled, studied, traversed. But always in threes. Why always in threes? The Trinity.

The answer escaped her as she sat staring into the sky, but she would keep looking, and if there was a way to fly solo, she would find it. For now she kept gazing up at the heavens, her thoughts flowing out among the stars.

Coda

C ris looked out the window at his daughter as she sat sipping her tea and staring up at the stars. He had waited for her to return. Had waited all these years because he knew she needed that closure. That knowledge that she had been successful and had rescued him from the past.

But now it was time for him to move on. It had taken all of his will, all of his strength over the years to stay in the present moment. He had waited for Maya, but he could wait no longer.

He thought of his experiences. How he had been one with the universe. How he had touched the moon and the stars. Experiences like that change a person. They changed him in ways that others could not comprehend if they had not experienced them themselves. When Cris was repairing the rift, he awakened, and he realized that he had to move on. His journey here was complete. He had to move on, to follow in his grandfather's footsteps, to chart his new path. Tears were streaming down his face. He was sorry that he must go, but he could not hold back any longer. He was meant to wander across the universe and across dimensions, to be lost and found again and again.

Cris looked deep into himself while opening completely to the universe. As he did, he began to glow brighter and brighter, almost as if the universe were shining from within him. He spoke aloud to the empty room, "I love you both."

In that moment, Cris turned to pure light. He shone brightly, like the light of a million suns. But even as the light grew in intensity, his form could still be seen as he merged back into the universe. As he set off upon his next journey, he looked with his inner sight at each of them one last time, and with a final flash of pure light, he was gone.

In the sudden physical void created by his departure, there remained joy. And love.

49596176R00074